KEEP BEACH CITY WEIRD

BY RONALDO FRYMAN
WITH ASSISTANCE FROM MATT BURNETT & BEN LEVIN

An Imprint of Penguin Random House

FOR JANE, MY OHIMESAMA—RF

CARTOON NETWORK BOOKS
Penguin Young Readers Group
An Imprint of Penguin Random House LLC

Penguin supports copyright. Copyright fuels creativity, encourages diverse voices, promotes free speech, and creates a vibrant culture. Thank you for buying an authorized edition of this book and for complying with copyright laws by not reproducing, scanning, or distributing any part of it in any form without permission. You are supporting writers and allowing Penguin to continue to publish books for every reader.

STEVEN UNIVERSE, CARTOON NETWORK, the logos and all related characters and elements are trademarks of and © Cartoon Network. (s17). All rights reserved. Published in 2017 by Cartoon Network Books, an imprint of Penguin Random House LLC, 345 Hudson Street, New York, New York 10014. Manufactured in China.

Photo credits: (yellow paper, ripped notebook paper, ripped graph paper) © A-R-T-U-R/Thinkstock; (torn paper edges) © -strizh-/Thinkstock; page 43 (cow silhouette) © Lindybug/Thinkstock.

Additional illustrations by Ben Levin.

ISBN 9781101995150

10 9 8 7 6 5 4 3 2 1

KEEP BEACH CITY WEIRD

DISPATCHES OF TRUTH FROM THE BEACH CITY UNDERGROUND

Beach City. It may look like just another East Coast beach town, but take off your sunglasses and you'll see the WEIRD: otherworldly creatures, paranormal phenomena, a restaurant that puts *fish* on *pizza*, and of course, ME! Ronaldo Fryman! The weirdest person in all of Beach City! (My friend Steven Universe and the Crystal Gems are a close second.) I've dedicated my life to documenting all that is weird on my blog, *Keep Beach City Weird*. If you haven't heard of it, you're probably one of the many publishers that rejected my book proposals. I wanted to compile my findings in a book to help spread the TRUTH! It seems the literary establishment is too afraid to compile my findings into a book to spread the TRUTH, so I've published it myself! Well, my dad helped a little bit, too . . . by paying for it. In exchange for the funding, I had to write in some ads for his fry shop. But I assure you, I did not let corporate advertising threaten the journalistic integrity of my investigations. (Thanks, Dad!).

What follows is my life's work. Prepare yourself for weird beyond your weirdest imagination.

WEIRD MONSTERS

Beach City is home to some truly weird wildlife – WILD being the operative word! Our local cryptozoological specimens go way beyond your typical two-headed snakes and squirrels that can shoot lasers out of their eyes. Here is just a small sampling of the weird creatures I've cataloged in my many expeditions.

RADIOACTIVE CENTIPEDE

Here's one bug problem I don't think an exterminator will be able to handle – unless they're packing a BAZOOKA! There have been several sightings of this creepy crawler on our beaches, each one slightly different from the last. Some people even say they've seen one that looked humanoid!

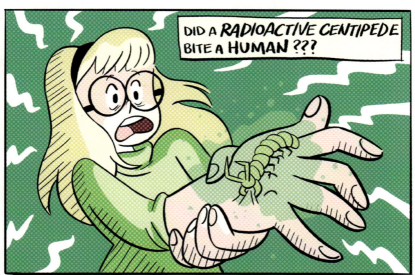

THE SCREAMING WORM

Its loud screeches caused earthquakes – and really hurt my ears. What was this monster worm after? Maybe it was the last of its kind, looking for a mate. Or maybe it was just running from something worse, like . . .

A GIANT Bird!!!

These airborne beasts will invade our regular-size houses, which they see as giant-size bird houses, forcing us underground to live with, that's right, the giant WORMS. Beach City – take down your bird feeders!

THE FLOATING MEGA PUFFER FISH

What is scarier than a beach ball? Well, I guess a lot of things, but one of those things would definitely be a beach ball COVERED IN SPIKES!

This oversize aquatic monstrosity was probably the most dangerous fish I've ever seen. Except for this one fish stick I ate that sent me to the hospital. It was a lot like the Floating Mega Puffer Fish: really pointy. Now that I think about it, I might have just eaten a piece of wood that fell into the deep fryer.

GIANT WOMEN FROM THE SEA

Over two hundred years ago, Mayor Dewey's great-great-great-GREAT-grandfather, William Dewey, and his first mate, Buddy, set out to find unexplored land. What they found instead was PERIL! Disastrous weather, towering waves, and perhaps worst of all, a sea monster! But lo – they were saved by a magical GIANT WOMAN FROM THE SEA!

She gently placed Dewey down on the shore, and that's where William Dewey decided to build Beach City. Nobody knows where this goddess came from, but some say the cliffside above Steven's house bears her visage. Probably no connection.

Offering wheelie shoe delivery service!
Delivered in 120 minutes or your meal is free!

But just last year, our shores were visited by yet *another* Giant Woman from the Sea. She totally demolished what seemed to be a very promising seaside gym that Steven and his dad had set up. Could this be the other Giant Woman's EVIL twin sister? Or her evil twin . . . granddaughter?! I hope they meet one day and battle it out. And then maybe I can ride around in one of their giant hands and be a super-cool sidekick!

MUTANT WATERMELON GUYS

Like most bad stories, this one started at a farmer's market. I bought one of these Mutant Melon Guys from Steven and tried to perform a watermelon autopsy to see what secrets lurked inside, and if they were seedless. But before I could make my first incision, I was attacked by a whole gang of Mutant Melon Guys! I guess that's the danger of genetically engineered food: It might punch you in the face. But who am I to complain? Sure, those watermelons beat me up, but they only cost five bucks apiece. What a deal!

We promise to NEVER bring out that Frybo costume again.

ZOMBIE LIMBS

There have been sightings of these strange creatures lurking on the outskirts of Beach City, wandering onto roads, hand-standing through forests, and lurching into backyard BBQs. Reports say they have no heartbeat. No heartbeat plus lurching can only equal one thing: zombies!

The only way to stop a zombie is to remove the head – but what if they don't have heads?! I'll have to seriously rethink my zombie apocalypse flow chart.

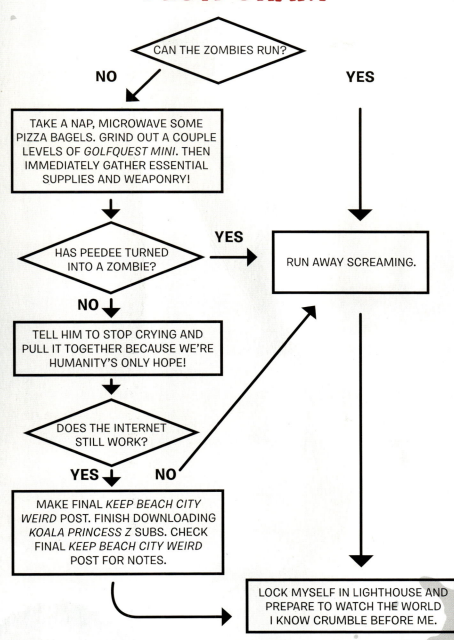

ENDANGERED WATER YETIS

For years I have been warning people about the dangers of global warming, and for years I've been ignored. But now that the ice caps have begun to melt, people are finally feeling the true effects of climate change: YETI INVASIONS.

The melting of their natural habitats has driven these abominable, but noble-able, arctic monsters onto our beaches. That's why I'm campaigning to turn the Beach City Ice Skating Rink into a preserve for these proud beasts.

EXTINCT? NOT YETI! THERE'S STILL TIME!

Please, help me turn the Beach City Ice-Skating Rink into a nature preserve for the endangered Water Yetis. These majestic beasts need our help and they'd make a great addition to the Boys & Girls Hockey League!

THE COLOSSAL CRAB

I happened upon this crustacean kaiju while I was filming my documentary, *Rising Tides/Crashing Skies: Danger on the Boardwalk: The Truth About the Most Dangerous Boardwalk: A KBCW Investigative Documentary*. It was a dangerous situation: The Colossal Crab was pinching its giant pincers and the Gems were shooting lasers at it, but I didn't let that stop me from standing fifty yards away while my brother filmed it. I'm such a brave journalist. And I guess Peedee was pretty brave for holding the camera.

The Crystal Gems disposed of the crab beast, but I think we all know who the *real* hero was that day – investigative reporting.

READ WHAT AUDIENCES HAVE TO SAY ABOUT THIS GRITTY EXPOSÉ ON DELMARVA'S WEIRDEST TOWN.

"I'm in this!"—Nanefua

"I give it five stars! Including the one on my shirt!"—Steven

"So, this is what you've been doing with your paychecks?"—Fryman

"Wow. This is so professional, Ronaldo."—Sadie

"YOU made this?!"—Lars

"Ocean Town has a much more dangerous boardwalk! We have half as many rusty nails as they do."
—Mayor Dewey

SNAKE PEOPLE OR SNEEPLE DEBUNKED

I used to think that Snake People, or Sneeple, were the venomous masterminds behind every conspiracy. I was convinced that they were pitting us mammals against each other with elections, sports, and anime message boards to keep us from finding out the TRUTH – that they control our government at the highest levels!

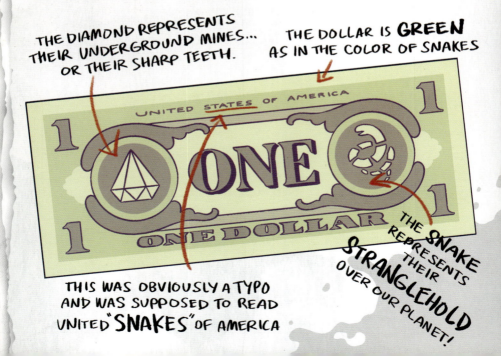

THE DIAMOND REPRESENTS THEIR UNDERGROUND MINES... OR THEIR SHARP TEETH.

THE DOLLAR IS GREEN AS IN THE COLOR OF SNAKES

THE SNAKE REPRESENTS THEIR STRANGLEHOLD OVER OUR PLANET!

THIS WAS OBVIOUSLY A TYPO AND WAS SUPPOSED TO READ UNITED "SNAKES" OF AMERICA

Oh, how wrong I was. Snake People – doesn't that sound ridiculous? The real threat is ROCK PEOPLE: aliens who want to hollow out the Earth so they can tow it back to their home planet in the Mud Galaxy.

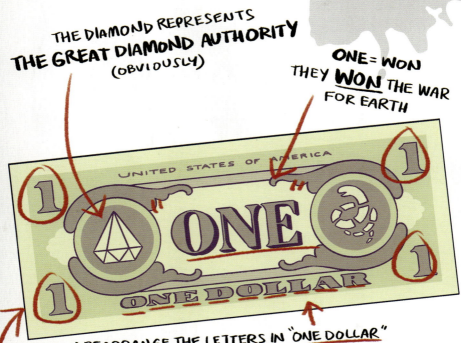

THE DIAMOND REPRESENTS **THE GREAT DIAMOND AUTHORITY** (OBVIOUSLY)

ONE = WON
THEY **WON** THE WAR FOR EARTH

IF YOU REARRANGE THE LETTERS IN "ONE DOLLAR" IT SPELLS "EL RONALDO" AKA "THE RONALDO" AKA ME! THE ONLY ONE WHO CAN STOP THEM!

1 × 4
↓
4 LETTERS
↓
R O C K
‾ ‾ ‾ ‾

THE BROKEN SNAKE REPRESENTS THE DESTRUCTION OF ORGANIC LIFE!

Although most out-of-towners visit Beach City for the beautiful ocean view, they should really be looking up to the SKY! For whatever reason, Beach City has become a top destination for INTERGALACTIC WEIRDNESS. From extraterrestrial encounters to unexplained cosmic phenomena, I have seen it all – and the stuff I haven't seen, I have made fairly educated guesses about. Shout-out to my research assistant – THE INTERNET!

VAMPIRE SPACESHIP

When this crimson space vessel entered our atmosphere, it nearly sucked the entire boardwalk up into the sky! But the real story of this spacecraft began over half a century ago.

The wild 1960s left America with an overabundance of vampires. So when scientists figured out how to get a man on the moon, they decided to bring along a bunch of Draculas and dump them into space. But the vampires were smart. They repurposed the landing module into a vampire spaceship and came back to Earth.

But why did the vampire spaceship come to Beach City? Well, yours truly has been working on a garlic french-fry recipe to ward off said Draculas.

I bet that vampire spaceship caught wind of my plan and tried to sabotage me! Nice try, space vampires!

YEAH, WE GOT CURLY!

ROCK PEOPLE SPACE PROGRAM

Usually UFOs come from space to visit Earth, but *this* flying object came from Earth and was going to space! The truth behind this super saucer is truly disturbing: The Rock People living inside the Earth have started a space program.

Beach Citywalk FRIES — BYOP: Bring your own potato—we'll turn it into fries!

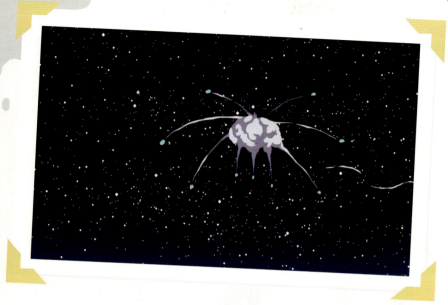

Luckily for us, their ship blew up before it could reach escape velocity. So it's safe to say their space program is pretty cruddy. Probably because they're all rocks. And rocks are super heavy and probably hard to get out of orbit.

Based on the trajectory of the ship, it must have launched from somewhere nearby. That means an entrance to the subterranean Rock World is in the vicinity of Beach City! Be on the lookout for anything that might be hiding a giant hole that leads to the center of the Earth, like a big pile of branches or a giant Persian rug.

PINBALL PROBES

Several crops of strange spherical ships have appeared above Beach City. Their sizes range from "WHOA THAT'S BIG!!!" to "Aw, it's so cute." Certain experts of the weird (me) postulate that these are scout ships from the notorious Pinball Galaxy: a distant cosmic empire ruled by an oligarchy of Evil Intergalactic Pinball Wizards!

Beach Citywalk FRIES — They're the nachos of the boardwalk!

An invasion is surely coming, and there's only one way to protect ourselves – a giant-size Earth Flipper Defense Squad.

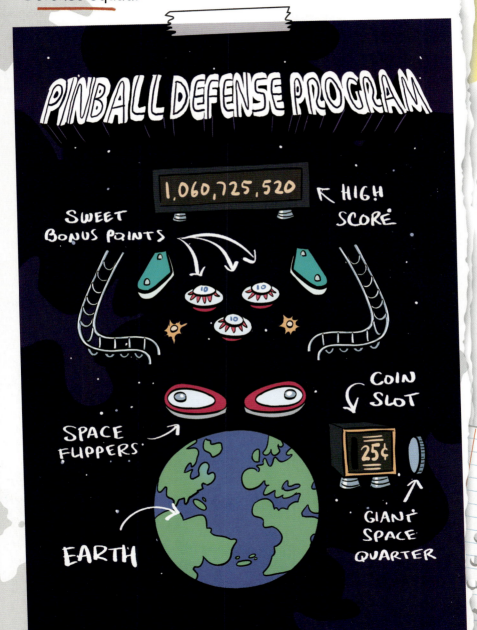

THE HAND SHIP

ACTUAL FOOTAGE

This high five from the heavens nearly destroyed our city. The town had to be evacuated. Everyone was scared, especially my li'l bro, Peedee.

ACTUAL FOOTAGE

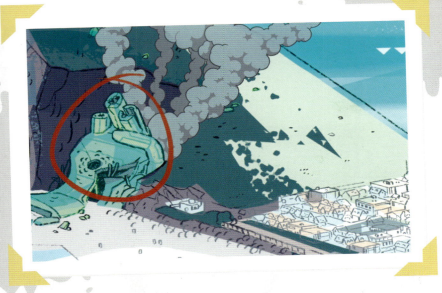

I had many theories. My favorite was that the hand was coming to snatch up humans for a human zoo in space! However, if you've seen my documentary, *Rising Tides/Crashing Skies: Danger on the Boardwalk: The Truth About the Most Dangerous Boardwalk: A KBCW Investigative Documentary*, you'll know that Steven informed me that this hand ship only wanted to grab one thing: the Crystal Gems.

I recently decided to do a follow-up interview with Steven to better understand why the Crystal Gems were being chased by body parts from space. I tried to transcribe it as best I could.

Only Steven gets the bits. Stop asking.

Ronaldo: Thanks for sitting down with me, Steven. And for this delicious lemonade.

Steven: You're welcome!

Ronaldo: So, tell me—why were the Gems being chased by this hand ship? [sips lemonade]

Steven: Well, I guess it all started almost six thousand years ago when my mom started a war with her home planet.

Ronaldo: [spits lemonade] What?! [coughing]

Steven: Oh no. Are you okay?

Ronaldo: [coughing] It's [cough] all over my laptop!

Steven: I'll get some paper towels!

Ronaldo: [cough] And could you get me some more lemonade? [cough]

Steven: Okay, here you go. So this one Gem, Peridot, was trying to come back to Earth, but we kept stopping her—

Ronaldo: [coughing] [sips lemonade] [more coughing]

Steven: Are you sure you're okay?

Ronaldo: Yes. [violent coughing]

Steven: Maybe we should do this another time . . .

[At this point in the interview my laptop shorted out.]

"Beach Citywalk Fries is [. . .] a [. . .] restaurant in [. . .] Beach City."
—*The Delmarva Post* review section

GUITAR DAD!!!

One day while walking on the boardwalk, this T-shirt came flying down from space and hit me in the head!

It bears the image of an alien being known as Guitar Dad. He appears to have the power to turn sonic energy into electricity. And he looks totally ripped!

Why was I chosen to receive this message? If I put it on, will this transdimensional textile send me across the galaxy or teach me to play sick riffs? Or is it a clever ploy to destroy all of humanity? A soft, cotton-polyester embrace that will disintegrate me into DUST? I'll never know, because it's a youth medium. If you're reading this, Guitar Dad, I wear an extra-large! No V-necks, please!

CROP CIRCLES

An act of intergalactic graffiti courtesy of the Diamond Authority! You'd expect aliens to want to turn this planet into a colony to harvest its resources for the purpose of creating more aliens, but they only seem interested in pranking us! What's next? Prank calls asking if the Earth's refrigerator is running? Gluing a quarter to the floor in front of the vending machine in the White House? Putting a whoopee cushion in our planet's orbital path?

Also, if you're wondering how I got this photo, I just set a timer on my phone's camera and threw it really high in the air.

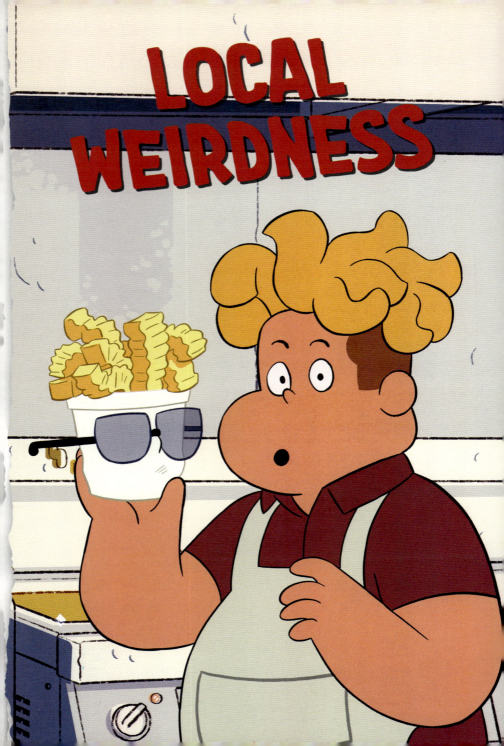

Not all of the weird things in Beach City come crashing down from space or crawling out of the sea. Some of the strangest beings and phenomena I've ever encountered call the boardwalk their home! Even the most average Boardie has experienced some kind of paranormality. Here is a selection of some of Beach City's finest homegrown, organic weirdness!

THE CRYSTAL GEMS

The Crystal Gems are the heroes who protect Beach City from being destroyed and from being boring! We've had our differences in the past. I did kidnap Steven Universe once, but *only because I thought he was a Snerson**!

I'd like to think we're all sort of the same: me, Steven, Square Head, Purple Girl, and Princess Nose. They fight with sweet weapons and magical powers. I fight using the written word, formatted for both laptops and mobile devices. They have a cool home base in an ancient magical temple. My base is a lighthouse that I'm not legally allowed to occupy. And, like all heroes, every morning we find danger on our doorsteps. In their case it was a giant spaceship shaped like a hand, but I've had this really scary librarian chase me down for an overdue book!

I guess that's just the burden that comes with being weird. Who knows? Maybe one day we'll team up to battle our most dangerous enemies together. Let's see that librarian kick me out of the Young Adult section when I've got Princess Nose by my side!

*Snerson is the singular form of "Sneeple."

Come out back and watch me slice up potatoes with my sick new katana!

WE WELCOME LOITERERS.

CAT FINGER FEVER

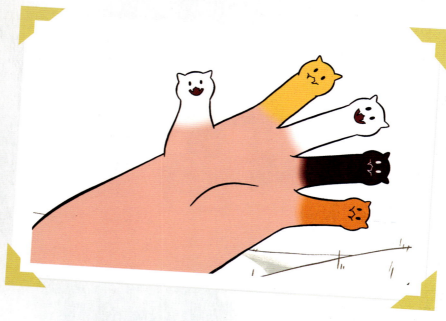

Steven showed up at the fry shop one day with a fist full of felines! This truly had to be seen to be believed. It appeared to be some adorable mutant strain of cat scratch fever. Not sure how contagious it was. Steven had it one day, but it was gone the next morning, so duration of infection is short. But I would be careful – I bet it's real hard to do stuff with cat fingers.

So how does one catch the finger variety of cat scratch fever? Steven doesn't hang out with any cats, other than his "Invisible Lion." But here's what I think . . .

IT'S A CONSPIRACY!!!

FACT: Steven used to love Cookie Cats. **OTHER FACT:** Steven got Cat Fingers. **SHOCKING CONCLUSION:** COOKIE CATS CAUSE CAT FINGERS!!!

That must be why Cookie Cats were discontinued! Seem impossible? Just follow the money.

Cookie Cats were made by Funtime Foods Inc., a subsidiary of the Amalgamated Dairy Industries of North America, a company owned by the Blergsdale Group.

And what is the Blergsdale Group's third-biggest-selling product? You guessed it – KITTY LITTER.

Those fingers aren't so cute anymore, are they?

FRYBO

Frybo used to be the frightening mascot of Beach Citywalk Fries. Then the suit magically became more frightening and attacked my family! Luckily, Steven stopped him – apparently by getting naked.

I feel really guilty about this whole thing. Not just because I was on my medically prescribed nap break when it happened, but because I may have caused this whole incident. You see, I was briefly into tuber-craft, a subsect of witchcraft devoted to potatoes and yams.

I had been experimenting on some potatoes in the back of the fry shop, offering them up as sacrifice to Yukonaclops, the Many-Eyed Potato God. He is the root that is buried deepest in the Earth that will grow in size until he is ready to be harvested, and in turn make a harvest of his own – a harvest of human souls!

Anyway, I MAY have briefly manifested Yukonaclops into this plane of existence and channeled the Elder Starch's spirit into the Frybo costume. Moral of this story: Don't read ancient, mysterious spells you find online out loud unless you know what you're doing!

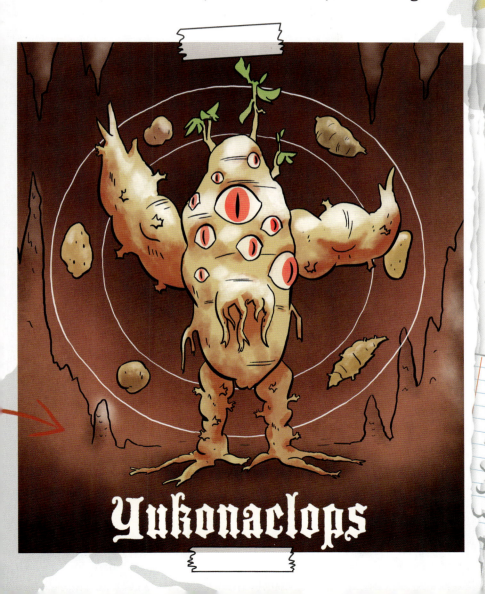

THE OLDEST MAN IN THE WORLD

Despite a lack of official recognition from any of the world-record-setting organizations, Beach City is home to the oldest man in the world. I mean, this guy is OLD. Somebody spotted him jogging through town one night, and man . . . he's got to be at least a thousand years old. How did he do it? Is jogging the secret? Does he only go out at night because he's a vampire?

Using a complex computer aging algorithim, I have re-created what the oldest man might've looked like when he was young.

Hey, he kind of looks like Steven!

THE MYSTERIOUS PINK LION

No need to go on a safari to see a jungle cat. If you visit Beach City, you just might catch a glimpse of this vibrant, yet elusive, mysterious pink lion.

Way cooler than that invisible lion Steven tried to show me one time.

He's a majestic relic of the Pink Pliocene epoch – a time when Beach City's ancient ecosystem included pink gazelles that were hunted on the Pink Plains by prides of pink lions and pink panthers alike.

Got too much salt? Buy some fries!

SPONTANEOUS COMBUSTION COUGH

Local sarcasm dispenser Lars Barriga came down with a case of spontaneous combustion cough. It's an extremely rare viral infection with one distinct symptom: FLAMES COMING OUT OF YOUR MOUTH!

Although Lars severely singed the boardwalk and his throat, I'd say he was lucky. In medieval times, people who came down with spontaneous combustion cough were mistaken for dragons and hunted by knights!

Back then, the prescription was swords!

GUACOLA: THE GROSSEST SODA EVER

Guacola: the world's first guacamole soda. I think they mean "the world's first soda that doesn't taste good!"

The preeminent beat boy of Beach City, Sour Cream, DJ-ed a rave sponsored by Guacola. It was a disaster. I was given a free sample of the stuff – or rather, someone hurled a can at my chest, and it nearly broke my sternum! This soda is so dense, it was like trying to drink a collapsed star! Or a can of fizzy guacamole.

Now, some say I'm a picky eater. Sure, for the first fifteen years of my life, I only ate pizza. But I ate it with a wide assortment of toppings – including *veggies*! But I gave Guacola more than a fair chance. I tried to drink it – gross! I tried to put it on chips – gross! I tried it with a waffle and a scoop of ice cream – TRIPLE GROSS. It's just disgusting.

Anyway, I definitely recommend you grab a can if you're in the Beach City area.

ONION

This kid is weird. Like, next-level weird. I'm weird, swamp children are weirder, earlobes are super weird, but Onion is just . . . I don't even know!

Once, he came to the fry shop and kept gesturing for me to give him ketchup packets. I gave him, like, fifty packets, and then asked him if he wanted fries. He just shook his head, handed me a photograph of myself from the third grade, and then ran away.

You can usually find Onion sitting on the docks or inside a vending machine at Funland Arcade. Say hello if you're in town!

Bring in definitive proof of Bigfoot's existence and get a free soda!

FUNLAND ARCADE

Every boardwalk worth its weight in saltwater taffy has an arcade. Beach City's own Funland Arcade is by far the best on the entire Eastern Seaboard.

Established over a century ago, the arcade was originally known as Frederick Ulysses Neptune's Land of Mechanical Oddities and Entertainment. It featured a robot fortune-telling machine, a coin-operated barbershop quartet, and something called the Kineto-Monkeyscope. Apparently, you could turn a crank and watch a filmstrip of a monkey wearing a top hat. Man, old movies were lame.

Today, Funland Arcade is filled with every arcade mainstay: *Battle Frog*, *Chrono Panic 4*, *Road Killer*, *Whackerman*, *Whackerman Jr.*, *Meat Beat Mania*, *Punch Buddy*, and my favorite – *Teens of Rage*. Probably because I am a teen who is full of rage at a world that doesn't understand how to pronounce "manga." Fun fact: *Teens of Rage* was originally created to deter break-dancing gang violence.

If you've got a little brother who's always following you around because he thinks you're so cool, just put him out front on the Jelly Jiggler or the Seahorse Tsunami. Peedee used to love those. They just make him look wistful now.

If you're from the Labor Department, my little brother is just a really short eighteen-year-old.

 HURRICANE TANTRUM

 ANGST PUNCH

 GROWTH SPURT

 FLYING GROWTH SPURT

 GET-OFF-MY-BACK FLIP

 DETENTION TAKEDOWN

 JIKO HAKAI-TEKINA KODO KIKKU

 INDIFFERENT SHRUG OF DOOM

RACE MOUNTAIN

Life moves a little slow in a sleepy seaside town like ours, but it moves pretty fast when racing down Race Mountain, AKA the Devil's Backbone, AKA the Devil's Laundry Chute, AKA the Devil's Poorly Planned Highway, AKA Old Man Carwreck's Road, AKA Municipal Maintenance Route 64!!!!

This spot on the outskirts of town is a staple of the East Coast underground car-racing scene. Thanks to its tight turns, racers can execute excellent drifting techniques on their downhill journey. I would totally ride this asphalt dragon myself, but I only have a scooter. Also, I lost my helmet, so I haven't even been able to scoot around.

The greatest race I ever witnessed was between long-time drifter, and big-time jerk face, Kevin and the mysterious Racer S.

Racer S rode in out of nowhere in the legendary '92 Dondai Supremo LX. But not even Racer S's superb braking skills and the Dondai's flawless limited-slip differential could topple Kevin's reign. He must be stopped. I must . . . save up for a really cool car.

Beach Citywalk FRIES

Reblog one of my *Keep Beach City Weird* posts for a 15% discount and to prove to my dad that WHAT I DO ON THE INTERNET IS IMPORTANT!

THE ABANDONED WAREHOUSE

What weird town would be complete without some weird abandoned buildings? By night, this old warehouse is home to some illicit teenage raves. But by OTHER nights, it is home to BEACH CITY UNDERGROUND WRESTLING, a semi-professional wrestling promotion run by Mr. Smiley!

Beach Citywalk FRIES — It's every potato's destiny to be sliced up and fried to a crisp. Don't let them die in vain.

Grapplers from all over Delmarva have been gathering here for years to battle for glory and honor, just like the samurai did, but in spandex. Even I have had the privilege of being part of BCUW's rich history. I competed in the squared circle as the Loch Ness Bloggster!

I got jobbed out to the Purple Puma before I could get a main event push, though.

BEACH CITY UNDERGROUND WRESTLING

BEACH CITY UNDERGROUND TAG TEAM WRESTLING CHAMPIONS

PURPLE PUMA & TIGER MILLIONAIRE

CULINARY TAG TEAM CHAMPIONS

BASTE FACE AND THE IRON SAUCIER

AFTER SCHOOL CHAMPION

ASSISTANT PRINCIPAL GENE McCORMICK

INTERDIMENSIONAL CHAMPION OF THE MULTIVERSE
GLOSSY WAYNE

OLD TIMEY SENIOR LEAGUE TAG TEAM CHAMPIONS
SARSPARILLA FRANK AND THE COLONIAL TERROR

X-TREME LEAGUE CHAMPION PRESENTED BY GUACOLA
THE OCEAN TOWN KID

WOMEN'S CAPED CRUSADER CHAMPION
TINA "TEN FINGERS" GONZALES

BROODING HILL

This scenic view is home to perhaps the weirdest thing ever: EMOTIONS!!! I come up here to feel stuff and brood. Brooding is like when something really serious is happening in your life, and you know nobody can ever relate to your problems, so you just stare off into the distance. And when someone asks what's going on, you just sigh and say, "Nothing." And then you look away from them, and let your frylocks blow in the wind. It looks super cool!

Don't have enough things to brood about? Here's a handy list I use in case I need an excuse to look upset. (Pro tip: If you don't have hair that can blow in the wind, I suggest getting a cape or a really loose shirt.)

THINGS TO BROOD ABOUT:

- YOUR FAVORITE ANIME CATCHING UP TO THE MANGA.

- THE FACT THAT YOU'VE NEVER SEEN A REAL-LIFE DINOSAUR, AND MAYBE... **YOU NEVER WILL!**

- PLOTHOLES.

- WHEN IT'S TOO COLD OUTSIDE TO WEAR SHORTS.

- CROWDFUNDING REWARDS TAKING **FOREVER**.

- WHEN A FAST-FOOD CHAIN DISCONTINUES YOUR FAVORITE MENU ITEM. **BRING BACK PEPE'S PEPPER PITA BURGER!**

- YOUR DAD MAKING YOU CLEAN THE CHARRED FRY BITS OUT OF THE DEEP FRYER EVEN THOUGH YOU DID IT **LAST NIGHT**, AND IT SHOULD BE YOUR **BROTHER'S** TURN TO DO IT!

- HAVING TO BEAR THE WEIGHT OF THE **TRUTH!**

- LOVE.

Sometimes I like to stab the big mushy ones with the sharp little crunchy ones.

ANCIENT GNOME CITY

The cliffsides of Beach City are definitely the town's holiest site . . . because they're literally full of holes! Dozens of them, cut right into the rock!

I've got two theories about what these could be.

Beach Citywalk FRIES — Family owned and operated . . . until aliens come and reveal that I am the heir to a galactic empire!

THEORY ONE: These holes used to be home to an ancient civilization of BEACH GNOMES!

Unlike their grumpy woodland cousins, Beach Gnomes loved fun in the sun. They wore tiny shell hats, rode hermit crab carriages, and made surfboards out of Popsicle sticks! Whenever a hungry seagull would circle by, the Beach Gnomes would quickly climb into their holes and pass the time by playing some sort of video game system made out of clams.

OTHER THEORY: Rattlesnakes live in the holes. I'm too scared to stick my hand in and find out which theory is correct.

HAUNTED LIGHTHOUSE/ LIGHTHOUSE GEM

Oh, you didn't think that our town was without a haunted historical landmark, did you? This lighthouse was constructed two hundred years ago, not to guide ships to port, but to keep them away! The operator of the lighthouse would shine the light directly into the eyes of approaching ships' captains, blinding them and forcing them to change course. Why? Well, as you've learned, things can get pretty weird in Beach City. Too weird for even the saltiest sailors.

When GPS was invented, the lighthouse became obsolete. It stood alone on that hill, waiting to be explored by only the bravest of explorers: the Beach City Explorer Club!

Me and my friend Lars (pictured on the left) ventured inside, hoping to make it our clubhouse. But when Lars tried to carve his name in the wall, the lighthouse fought back.

I took a picture of it, which Lars really did not want published. Check it out.

We got into a minor argument that sort of led to the end of the Beach City Explorer Club. Lars just wasn't ready to be weird, I guess. And so I stayed behind, all alone, and made the lighthouse my sanctuary for all that is weird.

Anyway, fifteen years later, Steven came over for a visit and we found out the lighthouse was possessed by a magical gemstone. Who would've known?

Beach City has been home to many strange occurrences. But each of these events has been either the subject of a massive cover-up or just dismissed as a weather balloon reflecting the moon or something. Local government may have tried to keep these incidents out of the headlines, but you can't keep the truth secret forever! Especially not when fearless individuals such as myself (or anyone else who posts online) are out there, reporting live from the scene of the WEIRD. Be warned: Gaining knowledge of these events may cause you to question the very nature of reality and drive you mad! But I put a lot of work into this book, so please keep reading.

GARDENS IN THE SKY

One spring day, a bunch of weird crystalline flowers showered Beach City at sunset. Where did this mysterious flora come from? Was it a seasonal gift from nature? Was it a signal for an invasion of bee people? Why do I ask so many questions in this book? Do I think asking an unending stream of questions is a way to engage my reader? Will I ever give you my actual theory for this? Yes!

Cloud seeding! The United States Air Force has been doing a little bit of sky gardening. They've hired scientists to literally plant seeds in the clouds to grow sky gardens! And these airborne botanical wonders make for the perfect distraction when their friends from the Andromeda galaxy want to swing by for a visit! Allow my diagram to explain.

HOW CLOUD SEEDING WORKS!

① TWO PLANES FLY OVER A CLOUD. ONE DROPS A PAYLOAD OF SEEDS, AND THE OTHER DOUSES IT WITH WATER.

② WITH PLENTY OF SUNSHINE THE FLOWERS BEGIN TO GROW!

③ THE BLOSSOMS ARE CARRIED AWAY BY THE WIND, AND THE PEOPLE BELOW ARE TREATED TO A BEAUTIFUL FLOWER SHOWER!

④ EVERYONE IS IN SUCH A GOOD MOOD, THEY DON'T NOTICE THE ALIENS!!!

Whatever caused this phenomenon, I was SUPER ALLERGIC TO IT. I was sneezing so hard, I almost vomited. But it was the perfect setting to re-create a scene from the anime *On the Mountain of My Innocence of My Youth*, a coming-of-age tale about a Japanese schoolboy who overcomes the death of his father by playing the oboe.

IT'S RAINING G.U.Y.S.

I am no stranger to the weird world of collectible toys. I was there for the notorious "Kids' Meal Riots" when Pepe's Burgers ran out of Dogcopter toys. And I personally ate forty boxes of Crying Breakfast Friends frozen dinners just so I could collect enough box tops for the Belgian Waffle variant figure.

But the great G.U.Y.S. invasion has to be the weirdest thing I've seen in all my days of toy collecting. You know, G.U.Y.S.? **G**uys **U**nder **Y**our **S**upervision! They're toys.

One day Beach City was FLOODED with THOUSANDS of Dave Guys! But as mysteriously as they appeared, they then disappeared without a trace! Where did they come from? Have toys figured out a way to reproduce? Or did a bitter collector try to flood the market and drive the price down on Dave Guys? If that's the case, the joke is on them, since Dave Guys weren't worth anything in the first place. Everyone knows Dave Guy is the worst!

THE DAY THE OCEAN DISAPPEARED

This was the day Beach City went from low tide to NO TIDE. Overnight, the ocean just disappeared, leaving nothing but a barren desert wasteland in front of our boardwalk.

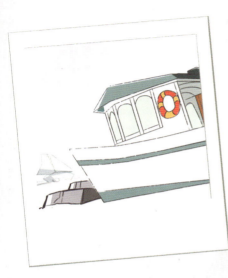

This could have been devastating to our town. I personally find Beach City full of fascinating oddities, but most of the sheeple who come to visit are just interested in the stupid ocean. And sheeple tourists are the driving force behind the town's economy. Luckily, Steven Universe somehow brought the ocean back.

But how could this have happened? The tides are controlled by the moon. So something must've shifted the moon's orbit to cause such a phenomenon. Could it be that the moon . . . HAS A MOON?!

THE GREAT BEACH CITY BLACKOUT

The power was OFF, but the weird was ON!

Mayor Dewey told everyone in town it'd be back on by sundown, but HE WAS LYING! He also told my dad that it was just some routine maintenance work. He was probably LYING about that, too! Because he was clearly being paid off by the GLOWSTICK LOBBY!

With rave attendance down, BIG GLOWSTICK needed a way to pump their wares into the American consumer's hands. And what better way than with a nationwide BLACKOUT?

From now on, when I dance, I'm using TORCHES ONLY.

WHEN PERIDOT BROKE TV

I was just in the middle of watching *Mighty Monster Card Traders: Shuffle Quest* and then there was a bunch of static and then THIS was on my TV!!!!!

This green girl had somehow managed to hijack all television frequencies to send out a mysterious distress call. She called herself "Peridot" (although I believe it's pronounced "Peridot"), and she was making a plea for someone named Yellow Diamond. Could it be? Diamond Authority Theory confirmed???

THE GREAT DIAMOND AUTHORITY

Polymorphic sentient rocks, or "Rock People," live in a strictly hierarchical society.

Rock People society is ruled by THE DIAMONDS: the most precious of the precious gems, and the TOUGHEST! Diamonds can cut through almost anything, so obviously nobody wants to mess with them.

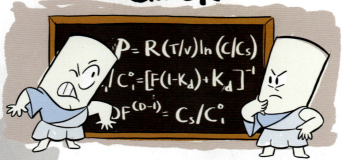

Below the Diamonds are the CHALK class. They're the philosophers and scientists of Rock People society. Chalkies, as they're affectionately known, use their heads to write complicated math equations and poems on chalkboards.

SLATE & GRANITE

GRANITE and SLATE are the workers of Rock People society. They build the rock cities — out of themselves!

ROCK CANDY

Rock People reproduce by growing ROCK CANDY BABIES in the vast sugar caves beneath the surface of their home planet. They may look sweet, but tastes can be deceiving.

CLODs

At the literal bottom of Rock People society are **CL**umps **O**f **D**irt, or CLODs. Nobody cares about CLODs.

See also: DEBUNKED: Snake People or Sneeple

CLUSTER QUAKES

A series of earthquakes SHOCKED and SHOOK Beach City! It felt like something was shaking the Earth at its very CORE. And the quakes came in CLUSTERS. There would be a bunch of tremors at once, and then they would stop. That's why I've dubbed them "Cluster Quakes."

I e-mailed my cool nickname to a couple of seismology publications, but they all told me that earthquakes don't need names. Only meteorologists waste their time naming tropical storms and hurricanes and stuff. Man, seismologists sure hate meteorologists.